ADRAMMELECH

Born of "Petrifying Well (°)",
a natural well where everything
can petrify
(°) .- English town of Knaresborough in Yorkshire.

Raised and educated by his father,
he he he grew up watching the rise
of life on earth; next to
of his tutor's creations ...

With the sole purpose, the
get more and more knowledge
to collect in the "Great
Library "of his father.

One Night, not long ago.
Adramm was curious about
the wisdom of "King Solomon"
and he started looking for answers ...

(°) .- Ophthalmologist, Mathematician Ingles (1527-1609).

(°) .- French Writer (1862-1923).

Well no ... This book is very good!
Who dares to enter without permission
to my father's house? In fact it is
impossible...
But Afternoon ...
I will notify my father that I will be
studying one of his prized books,
and what to ...
... get some economic funds. So
be able to sustain my new research
and find out if something strange has
happened in the library.
Hours later in his own shelter ...
This book was missing from my collection
personal; archaic and exoteric.
Here you will have a
prominent place.
* Un Querubín

"Clavicles of Solomon 2020", also available to our readers. By Leonardo Gudiño

An overwhelming person ...

"... They did not understand it, and Rehoboam ..."
It is witchcraft! Rehoboam has pact with the devil!
Run away! loves us cast a spell on everyone!
"... He was accused of practicing the Witchery. So that..."
There is nothing that you can say in your defense.
"... He was expelled from the university and I destroy his robot ... "
IMBECIES!
They don't understand anything!
"... I go to Louvain, where I engage friendship with Mercator (°) "
(°) .- Gerhadus Mercator (1512-1594). Celebrate Cartographer Dutch.
"... From whom he obtained 2 terrestrial globes of gold and various navigation instruments covered with silver that he made available of the English crown, so as not to be executed ... "
With this, my forgiveness is assured.

"... In antwerp. In 1563, he found incomplete a copy of the steganography of ABAD TRITEMO (°) ... "
(°) .- Abbot Juan de Heindenberg (1462-1516). The work consisted of 8 volumes about hypnotism to long distance, linguistics, math, cabal and parapsycology. It was destroyed and apparently no full copy of the book.

"... On May 25, 1581, within its studies of steganophy ... "
Open the door ...! The steps are taken!
"... I managed to open the door to another dimension and ... "
Who are you? That so you know on earth, the way to call us?
I am friend. We can be

"... Established contact with a being from another dimension, who he called ... "
You are Hummita. I know

Contact has already been established. We want you to know, if you are worthy of the.

"... And the strange being ..."
In proof of friendship, I give you this universal window ...
Strange mirror.

Looking at it you will see Other worlds.
It's possible?

You can establish contact with minds of beings that do not populate you planet
Extraordinary!

I have given you the most object valuable that has ever had the human race...

Use it for her benefit. That's what I give you for that.
Hears! Do not go. Listen to me!

"... Rehoboam used the mirror in multiple occasions ... "
What an extraordinary experience!

"... And he became an authority on chemistry, physics, optics, mechanics, linguistics ... "
... So studies have shown!

"... Also, and after getting more knowledge he was able to do the first book on "The clavicles of Solomon" ... "

"... Perhaps the most important thing besides, is that I left well established the language spoken by those to whom the he called Ummitas ... "
Everything is covered.

The Enoquinan language already it's easy for me to understand

"... I leave elements that allow to know now the secrets of his father Solomon .. "

"... Even so there were people who did not trust a such a peculiar individual ... "

"... Many secrets were lost when, In 1597, a mob destroyed and burned his house ... "
KILL THE WITCH!

"... 4 thousand esoteric books were lost there, 5 manuscripts and many knowledge notes of other dimensions ... "
DAMN! DAMN! I WILL REVENGE!!!

"... Only the mirror, a few notes and writings were saved on the original clavicles that are preserved in the British museum, as evidence of the existence of that strange man who died miserably in 1608 ... "
I will return and my revenge IT WILL REACH THEM ALL!

Do you know something Temelus? Time to go to that museum, my Dad has all the other documents in the library that they were supposedly destroyed, and it's never enough!

The next day...
Yes Dad, I promise we will ransack the whole place. I just need what we have on the British museum.
What a good son, the plans are in architecture area, and by if he also uses the same Solomonic seals for luck.

And the next three weeks ...
Although the museum is well protected. I will seize all your objects.

Should I disable these alarms, or all will be lost.

After that I will get to this point and the main objects will be mine then the cherubs will go for the rest.

And a month later ...
We will land within twenty minutes, Temelus.

Then...
RRRRR!

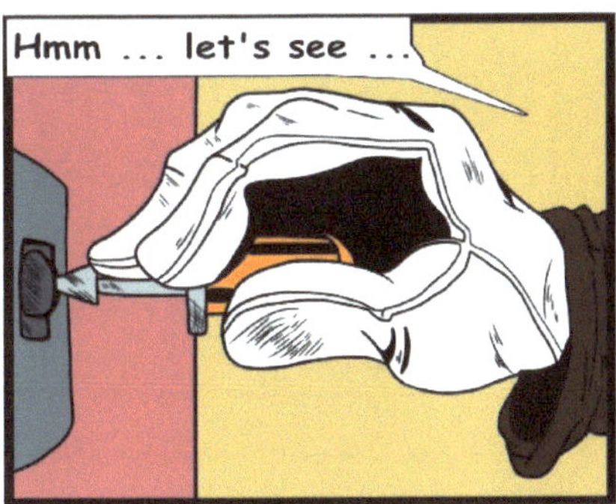
Hmm ... let's see ...

AHA! Here is the driver of ventilation for the system.
The manual says that no one can enter through the ...

... But you tell lies, right Temelus?
You will walk up and down until to rescue you.

It is great to be able to work without any fear ...

Now Daddy's Cherubs, using this locator will be able to open the portals to to be able to enter and loot until the last piece

... Although I'm sure if there were no alarms to overcome, my profession would lose its alluring ...

But later ...
Come on, Temelus. All went well! You know what to use portals or my powers of "Umbrakinesis" is not fun, it's better the old way ...

Your hair charged with electricity interfered with the entire electrical system uh, you made all the alarms useless.

Nights later
In the shelter...
Moonless night, it seems ideal for this experiment.

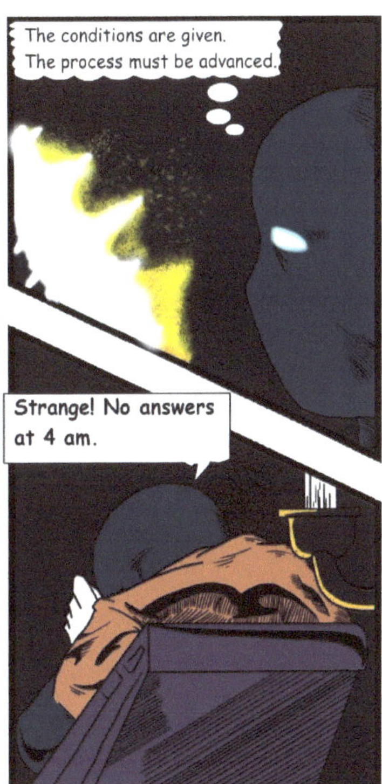

The conditions are given.
The process must be advanced.
Strange! No answers at 4 am.

However...
I'll change the orientation of the mirror...

And suddenly ...
I made it! There is the first embodiment!

(°) .- Means Obstacle of any class.

That mirror and all the documents from your library open the way to true pure knowledge!
So is. Only the most minds bright we must have room in her...
I see, your intentions ...
... No one else will enter that dimension, nor to the library a time we have it. We are just a select few ...
... We will accept no one else.
DAMN!
Your! You can't touch mirror! Wasn't it yours ?!
The bridge between both dimensions it's ... imperfect. My body mass could not get through, and only once my astral projection.
Yes, of course ...

One piece of advice, don't challenge my power that has passed the passage of centuries !!! I am the son of Solomon!
It is not me who challenges him. It's you who comes to attack me in the name of that power what do you say you have.

You entered my father's house without permission that is unforgivable, that's why I claim this mirror for him!

Who are prisoners in the dimension of thought we need it To return to what was ours Give it up voluntarily. Obey!
Your time, and kingdom passed. If I am not enough for you, It is not my fault...

... I won't give it to you. It's written that the past must not return to take a place in the present.
We will finish you off mortal! To your death we will have back.

I am not afraid of you, Rehoboam! Never you will have the mirror again and less the Great Library!
It will be useless to change the mirror orientation. I already drink the way. I will never lose it again! Your library will be ours too !!!

From that night on. The life of Adrammelech he found himself in constant danger ...
Sorry honey it's another curse.
Sorry honey it's another curse.
CRACKS!

SUUUOS!
Luckily, don't wear yet nothing to the library though I have 4 lost addresses with this...

... In increasingly dangerous actions ...

I will dedicate myself to studying everything thoroughly what I have on hand ... so I'll fix the problem.
Here I have to have the answer, I will not take them to my Father's house.

Near the mirror there seemed to be no danger ...
Sure enough, I think I found what I was looking for.

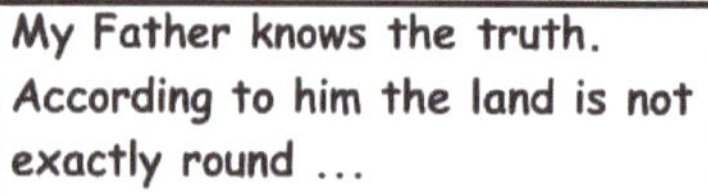

My Father knows the truth. According to him the land is not exactly round ...

That. What any elementary school kid should know it is the result of a very advanced knowledge from my dad.

It is claimed that the earth is composed of several spheres overlapping, and aligned ...

... Along other dimensions and realities. Another concept too advanced for any age!

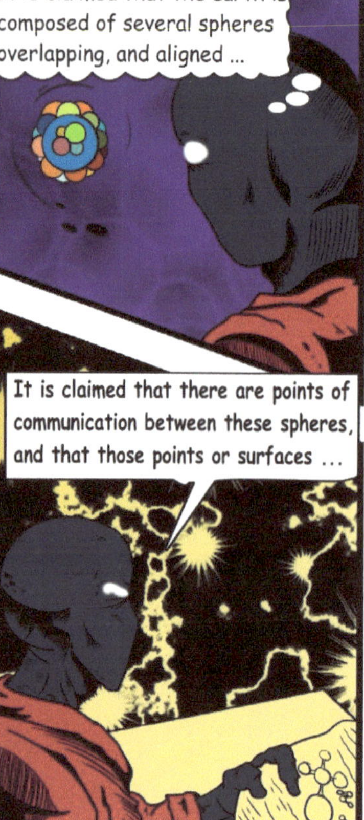

It is claimed that there are points of communication between these spheres, and that those points or surfaces ...

... They are actually doors to other dimensions, 5 realities and towards worlds different from ours.
Greenland, China, Mexico, Russia, are communication surfaces of our planet with other dimensions ...

...So that. That frozen region extends to infinity in time, space and dimensions unknown for us.

Greenland? So that's where I believe I must go to find my battle against Rehoboam ... It is better than here in Mexico.

Don't look for this contest. But if the son of Solomon and his people want my death to seize the mirror. When fighting no I do nothing but defend myself.

Impromptu ...
So what did you discover ?!
CRACKS!

Why not? I'm so used to thinking how were you
But you were worth it of my studies!

Nor can you against us!
If my life comes between you and the library, I assure that ...
The next time we Let's see it will be the last. Why you will die and everything will be ours.
We will know very soon.

... They will never have it, because I will defeat them. The mirror no it matters to me!
YOU ARE BRAVE! WORSE FOR YOU!!

For several days he prepared ...

I will face the brightest minds of all the times...

... In the only way possible ...

... What you learn in steganography of the Abbot Tritemo. It will be useful to me ...
Nobody, according to Tritemo. Can hypnotize me or impose his will on me if ...

... I hold steady in my mind the knowledge that I have acquired.
I must strengthen my body until it is immune to low temperatures, cute.
What do you expect with that sir?

(°) .- Mythical book that, according to the Egyptian betrayal. Contains the knowledge of all secrets of heaven and earth.

(°) .- Company: Action or task that involves effort and work, not necessarily a business or capital site.

Hours later, in Greenland ...
The triangle of supreme power protect me from the elements ...

Reflection angles will increase the force of light ...

Pure light that will illuminate the passage of who find this door ...

Final key to the eternal mystery. It fulfills the purpose for which you were created!
When, simultaneously, the candles suddenly lit up, a explosion of light that bathed the mirror ...
POP
POP
POP
Nothing can stop ya the final process. They or me, there is no alternative!

OUTSIDE THE TRIANGLE STALK ONE VIOLENT SWING ...
Things happen just like they were planned.
FUUOOSS!
Stop the advance of triangle or I will!
If they were sure of it they would not have to repeat it with so much frequency.
Gruesome monsters threatened kill Adrammelech
Cease your vain visions! You won't be able to scare me!
Suddenly...
The door has been opened. You convince yourself that you couldn't help it?
YOU WILL NOT BE ABLE TO BEAT US. OUR POWER IS INFINITE!
You can not do it. It has been open the door and alone my will will close it.

If you go in here, you won't come out again.
Here I come, Rehoboam. You called me!

You wished for my death without I wish you harm Now i go to you to settle differences.
You enter my field! You are lost Alien!

Welcome stranger, to the council of dignities!
You must be the scorpions that keep the knowledge; who's talking the book of Thot!
You know this advice I already decree your death!
I must finish with you to win to the Serpent of sin, which is the envy, fear, and vanity that they afflict Rehoboam.

(°) .- Hermetic book (1532).
It consists of one hundred astrological aphorisms.

28

"The Great Newfoundland", a great narrated adventure available in Ebook! by Leonardo Gudiño

BUT WHAT IS HAPPENING TO ME !!!
It was always like this, you didn't realize. Well now I'll use a little effort.

You know what the law is, Rehoboam doesn't we can coexist together though be in different dimensions.

You are defeated, Rehoboam! These halves will never come back To join!

I did what I have to do. The key to knowledge is mine. I'm here, ready to peek what I do not know.

Suddenly the wall of snow disappeared. and in its place was a paradisiac valley.
Be welcome, brother. You fought nobly, as you should, and you triumphed. Come here, you've shot down the barriers.

Time after. He didn't even know when or where. Adrammelech was flying over the English Channel. What did he see when the door of that room was opened? strange dimension? What unsuspected worlds discovered in that adventure? What treasures of wisdom did he receive from those who possess all the knowledge of the universe? Perhaps one day Adrammelech himself will provide us the answers to such exciting questions.
END?

ARGUMENT:
Leonardo Gudiño
SUPERVISION:
Leonardo Gudiño
ART:
Leonardo Gudiño
MX
HECHO EN
MÉXICO